LOOK AND FIND®

the AMAZING SPIDER-MAN®

LAYOUT ARTIST/ILLUSTRATION COORDINATOR: HOWARD BENDER
PENCILERS: HOWARD BENDER, RICH YANIZESKI, BRIAN CLOPPER, ALEX MORRISSEY, BRIAN BUNIAK
INKERS: DON HECK, MIKE ESPOSITO, MARIE SEVERIN
COLORISTS: NANSI HOOLAHAN, BRIAN BUNIAK, KEN FEDUNIEWICZ, TOM LUTH, TOM ZIUKO
COVER ARTIST: JEFF ALBRECHT STUDIOS

ILLUSTRATION SCRIPT DEVELOPMENT BY DWIGHT ZIMMERMAN

PUBLISHED BY
LOUIS WEBER, C.E.O.
PUBLICATIONS INTERNATIONAL, LTD.
7373 NORTH CICERO AVENUE
LINCOLNWOOD, ILLINOIS 60712

WWW.PUBINT.COM

LOOK AND FIND IS A REGISTERED TRADEMARK OF
PUBLICATIONS INTERNATIONAL, LTD.

8 7 6 5 4 3 2 1

ISBN 0-7853-5184-1

publications international, ltd.

I, MYSTERIO, HAVE UNLEASHED THE ULTIMATE PLAN! NOT ONLY WILL MY CRIME SPREE TURN NEW YORK INTO A CITY OF CHAOS, IT WILL ALSO END IN THE DEFEAT OF MY GREATEST NEMESIS, SPIDER-MAN! ALREADY HE'S HOT ON MY TRAIL, BUT ONLY BECAUSE OF THE CLUES I LEFT FOR HIM. WITH A LITTLE HELP FROM ME, HE MIGHT OFFER ME AN AMUSING CHALLENGE.

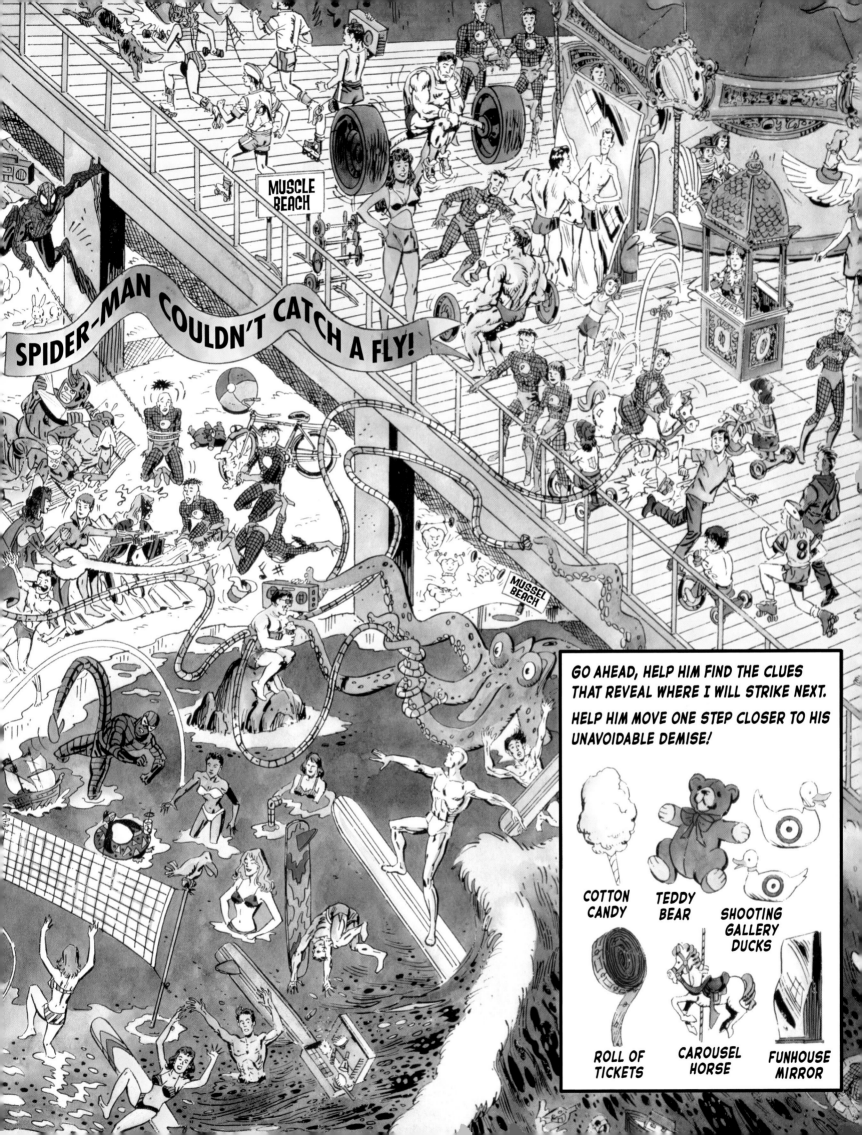

WHILE SPIDEY'S WORKING ON HIS PLAN, SEE IF YOU CAN FIND THESE THINGS THAT TELL WHERE MYSTERIO WILL GO FROM HERE.

THEATER MASKS

ACTOR

ACTRESS

COWBOY WITH LASSO

OPERA GLASSES

LION

TAXI

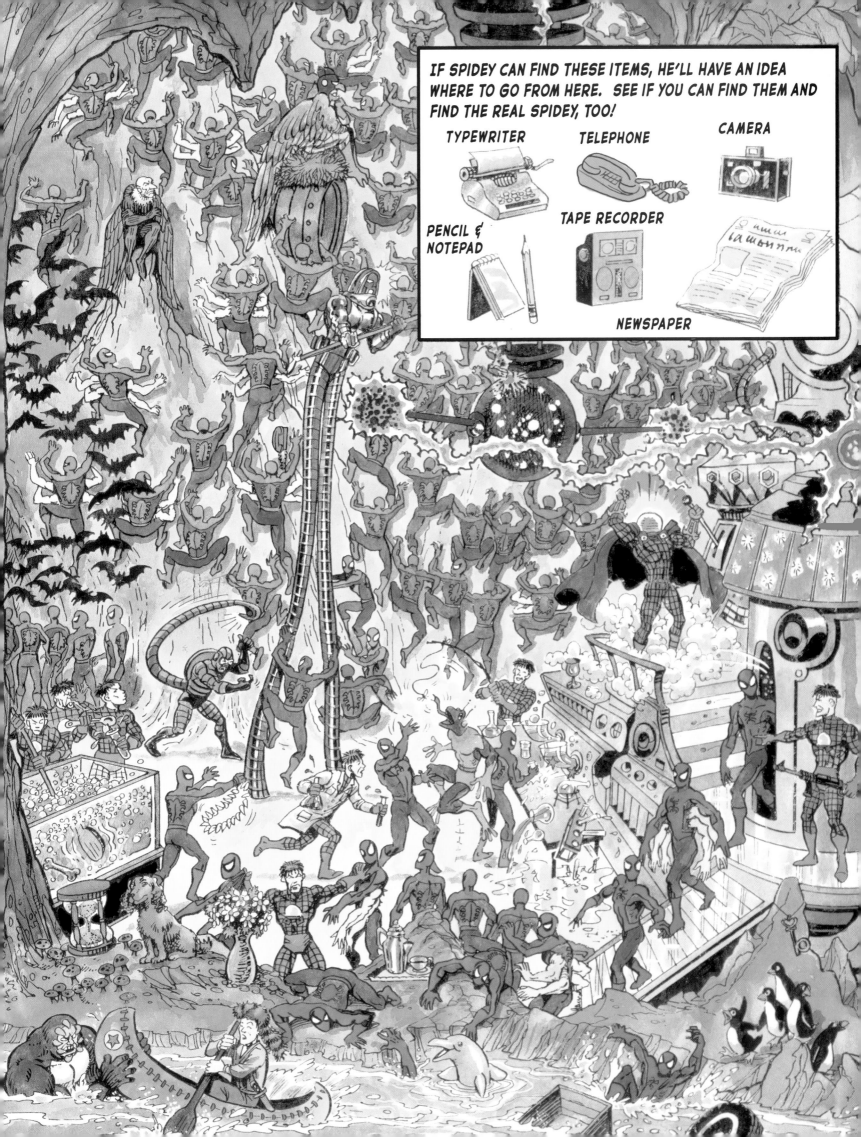

SEARCH THE STREETS OUTSIDE THE BUGLE BUILDING FOR MYSTERIO'S DEVICES, AND THEN HOPE OUR HERO CAN DISARM THEM BEFORE THEY GO OFF.

IN ALL THE CONFUSION BACK AT THE DAILY BUGLE OFFICE, PETER PARKER LEFT SOME THINGS BEHIND. SEE IF YOU CAN FIND THEM FOR HIM.

- ❑ A SPIDER-MAN MASK
- ❑ A SPIDER-MAN SHIRT
- ❑ SPIDER-MAN TIGHTS
- ❑ SPIDER-MAN GLOVES
- ❑ SPIDER-MAN BOOTS
- ❑ SPIDER-MAN WEB SHOOTERS
- ❑ A CAMERA

THE MASTER OF ILLUSION AND SPECIAL EFFECTS HAS MISPLACED SOME OF HIS GEAR. GO BACK TO THE BEACH AND FIND THESE THINGS MYSTERIO USED TO PLAY HIS TRICKS.

- ❑ A MAGIC WAND
- ❑ A DECK OF CARDS
- ❑ A TOP HAT
- ❑ A WHITE RABBIT
- ❑ A MAKE-UP KIT
- ❑ A PAIR OF HANDCUFFS
- ❑ A FAKE MUSTACHE

THE SCARLET WITCH HAS LEFT SOME OF HER ITEMS OF SORCERY BACK AT THE AMUSEMENT PARK. HELP HER TRACK THEM DOWN BEFORE THEY FALL INTO THE WRONG HANDS.

- ❑ A WITCH'S HAT
- ❑ A BROOM
- ❑ A BLACK CAT
- ❑ A BOOK OF MAGIC SPELLS
- ❑ A FROG PRINCE
- ❑ A CANDLE
- ❑ TOADSTOOLS

MATT MURDOCK LIKES TO SPEND QUITE A LOT OF TIME AT THE BALLPARK. GO BACK THERE AND TRY TO FIND THESE DARING AND DEVILISH ITEMS.

- ❑ DAREDEVIL LOGO
- ❑ DAREDEVIL'S BATON
- ❑ A GRAPPLING HOOK
- ❑ A PAIR OF SUNGLASSES
- ❑ A PITCHFORK
- ❑ A PAIR OF BOXING GLOVES

ALL THIS CRIMINAL ACTIVITY IS MAKING FROG-MAN HUNGRY. HAVE A LOOK AROUND RADIO CITY MUSIC HALL FOR THESE SUCCULENT TREATS HE'D LOVE TO GOBBLE UP.

- ❑ A SPIDER
- ❑ A FLY
- ❑ A BEETLE
- ❑ A CATERPILLAR
- ❑ A BUTTERFLY
- ❑ A GRASSHOPPER
- ❑ A WORM